A Purr-fect Pumpkin

Swim into more adventures!

PuRRMaiDS

MeRMiCORnS

A Purr-fect Pumpkin

by Sudipta Bardhan-Quallen

illustrations by Vivien Wu

A STEPPING STONE BOOK™
Random House 🏠 New York

To Kaity-cat, a purr-ific friend!

Text copyright © 2022 by Sudipta Bardhan-Quallen
Cover art copyright © 2022 by Andrew Farley
Interior illustrations copyright © 2022 by Vivien Wu

Visit us on the Web!
rhcbooks.com

Educators and librarians, for a variety of teaching tools, visit us at
RHTeachersLibrarians.com

Library of Congress Cataloging-in-Publication Data is available upon request.
ISBN 978-0-593-43305-8 (trade) — ISBN 978-0-593-43306-5 (lib. bdg.) —
ISBN 978-0-593-43307-2 (ebook)

Printed in the United States of America
10 9 8 7 6 5 4 3 2 1
First Edition

This book has been officially leveled by using
the F&P Text Level Gradient™ Leveling System.

1

It was almost time for Room Eel-Twelve's Paw-loween party. The purrmaids in the classroom were buzzing with excitement.

Most of them were.

One orange kitten named Coral was smiling just a little bit less than her classmates. A lot of the other purrmaids didn't notice. They were getting their squid-ink brushes ready to decorate jelly-o'-lanterns.

Luckily, there were two girls who could

tell that Coral was nervous. One was a kitten with silky white fur named Shelly. The other kitten, with black-and-white fur, was named Angel. They were Coral's two best friends. She could always count on them to know how she felt.

"Are you worried about the Paw-loween Festival, Coral?" Shelly asked, whispering.

Coral shrugged. "Not the whole fes-tival," she said. "I'm excited about most of it. Just the Haunted House makes me worry."

Angel reached out to squeeze Coral's paw. "You know we'll be with you the whole time, right?" she asked.

Coral nodded. "I know. And that makes me feel better." She picked up her brush and pointed it at their teacher. "But

I don't want to talk about it right now. Ms. Harbor is about to start."

At the front of the class, Ms. Harbor arranged a line of jelly-o'-lanterns on her desk. "Does everyone have a pumpkin jellyfish?" she asked.

"Yes!" the students replied.

"Wonderful!" Ms. Harbor exclaimed. "Now, here are some examples of jelly-o'-lanterns I've already painted. You can paint any kind of face you want on yours. But I always find it easier when I have some fin-spiration!"

Coral took a quick look at the jelly-o'-lanterns, but she really didn't need fin-spiration. She already knew what kind of face she wanted to paint. She started with a small triangle in the middle of the pumpkin jellyfish. She added two circles for eyes and two more triangles for ears. She drew a W-shape for a smiling mouth and some whiskers. Then she added the finishing touch—she painted some ear-rings on the triangle ears.

Coral sat back to take a good look at her jelly-o'-lantern. "It looks just like Ms. Harbor!" she said, laughing.

"It does!" Angel agreed. Then she

turned her pumpkin jellyfish for Coral to see. "Here's mine!"

Angel's jelly-o'-lantern looked terrifying! Instead of a smiling mouth, Angel had painted a mouth full of spiky teeth. She even added angry eyebrows!

"It's very scary," Coral said.

Angel grinned.

"Can I see yours, Shelly?" Coral asked.

Shelly nodded and moved out of the way. Her jelly-o'-lantern was very different from Coral's and Angel's. The eyes were two half-moon shapes and there was no nose. But the mouth was huge and open, and it seemed like the jelly-o'-lantern was screaming!

"Spooky!" Coral said.

"I agree," Ms. Harbor said, floating over to the girls. She checked out the three

jelly-o'-lanterns. Then she frowned. "This one looks like me," she said, pointing to Coral's pumpkin jellyfish.

"I know," Coral said. "You were my fin-spiration!"

But that just made Ms. Harbor frown harder. "Coral," she said, "are you saying I'm *scary*?"

Coral gasped. She hadn't meant to

upset her teacher! She tried to think of how to explain.

But then Ms. Harbor winked. "I'm just squidding," she said.

Coral let out a big breath. "I was worried!" she said. "Do you like it?"

Ms. Harbor smiled. "It's purr-fect. I know exactly where to put this in the Haunted House tonight."

"What?" Coral asked.

"Oh," Ms. Harbor said, "I still need to make an announcement." She grabbed Coral's jelly-o'-lantern and swam to the front of the classroom. "I forgot to tell all of you. Tonight is the Kittentail Cove Paw-loween Festival."

"Everyone knows that already," Umiko said.

Ms. Harbor nodded. "I'm going to take all of your jelly-o'-lanterns to finish decorating the Haunted House!"

"My uncle, the mayor, says it's going to be fin-tastic!" Adrianna said.

I hope so, Coral thought.

2

A new Haunted House was built every Paw-loween. The Cove Council held a contest to pick the best idea for the house. The students of Room Eel-Twelve were very proud of this year's winning team— which just happened to be the sea school teachers!

"I would love to see all my students there this year!" Ms. Harbor continued. "We filled it with extra-creepy fun!"

"And who doesn't love a good scare?" Adrianna joked.

Coral bit her lip. "I don't," she mumbled.

"You don't have to go to the Haunted House," Shelly whispered.

But Coral didn't want to be the only student in the class who didn't visit the Haunted House. Especially since Ms. Harbor worked really hard on it. She also didn't want to look like a scaredy cat in front of everyone. They might make jokes about her fears. Coral wasn't sure if they'd be nice jokes. "I'll be fine," she said.

"Can you tell us something about the Haunted House, Ms. Harbor?" Baker asked.

"Something other kittens won't know?" Taylor added.

Ms. Harbor giggled. "I shouldn't give

away any secrets," she said. "But if you *purr-omise* not to tell . . ."

"We purr-omise!" the students shouted.

"All right, then," Ms. Harbor said. "I'll tell you about my favorite room. It's the last room in the Haunted House, and it is filled with sea monsters."

Everyone cheered with excitement— except Coral. Sea monsters sounded really scary. *But now at least I have some warning,* she thought. She just didn't know if that was better.

The school day was about to end. The students were carrying their jelly-o'-lanterns up to Ms. Harbor's desk as they finished. "These are fin-credible," Ms. Harbor said. She turned to the students who were still working. "Do any of you need anything for your projects?"

"Actually," Cascade said, "I have a

question. Do we have any homework
tonight?"

Many of the students groaned. Most
of them were probably hoping Ms. Harbor would forget about homework. But
Coral thought it was a good question!

Ms. Harbor smiled and held up a paw
for silence. "I do have one thing for you

to do tonight," she purred. "Be brave and have fun! Have a Happy Paw-loween!"

That made the students cheer. Except Coral. She gulped. Ms. Harbor was asking for the one thing that would be hard for her. *Can I still have fun when it's so hard to be brave?*

☙ ☙ ☙

Coral, Angel, and Shelly swam home from sea school. Usually, the girls hung out together after school. But they had decided that their Paw-loween costumes would be a surprise. So they said good-bye when they reached Leondra's Square. "Remember," Shelly said, "we'll meet back here in half an hour."

Coral nodded and then raced away. She couldn't wait to show her costume to her friends. But first, she had to finish making it!

Coral yelled a quick hello to Mama and her little brother, Shrimp. Then she sped off to her bedroom.

Coral decided weeks ago that she wanted to be a fairy princess. She had been working on her costume for a long time. She wanted it to be very special. But she wasn't quite done.

Coral had gotten two coconut leaves from Mr. Bengal at Coastline Farm. She planned to turn them into fairy wings. But that meant they had to be sewn onto her fanciest, sparkliest dress. Unfortunately, Coral didn't know how to sew!

"Mama!" Coral shouted. "Can you help me, please?"

Mama swam to Coral's bedroom door. "What's going on?" she asked. "First, you rushed through the house. You barely said a word on your way in. Now you're shouting!"

"Sorry, Mama," Coral said. "I'm just in a hurry. I have to finish my costume so I can meet Shelly and Angel. The Pawloween Festival is tonight!"

"It's fine," Mama purred. "Can I help you sew those wings on?"

Coral grinned. Mama always knew exactly what she needed! "Yes, please!"

"I'll be right back," Mama said. She took the dress and the wings to her sewing room. Coral decided to work on the other parts of her costume while she waited for Mama. She found a glittery blue pencil. Then she glued a starfish on its tip to make a wand.

Now I need a crown, Coral thought. She found a gold headband in her drawer

and a bunch of tan tower shells. With a little more glue, her crown was almost ready. It just needed one final touch.

Coral opened the jewelry box on her table. Inside was her special crystal. She glued it to the center of the crown. "All done!" she purred.

"And I'm done, too," Mama said. She floated in the doorway of Coral's bedroom. She held out the dress with the wings attached. It looked absolutely fin-credible!

3

"Time to get dressed!" Coral exclaimed, laughing. She took the costume from Mama. "I'll be right out!"

Carefully, Coral slipped into her outfit. She placed the crown on her head and watched the crystal glitter in the light. She straightened the wings and picked up the wand. She checked her reflection in the mirror and grinned.

This is a paw-some costume, Coral

thought. She finally started to feel excited about the Paw-loween Festival.

Coral twirled through the house to show Mama her costume.

"You look like a purr-fect fairy princess," Mama said.

"Thank you!" Coral replied. "I can't wait to show everyone."

"I remember how fin-teresting the Paw-loween Festival can be for kittens," Mama purred. "I loved the Haunted House when I was your age."

Coral turned away quickly. She didn't want Mama to see her frown. Then Mama would know that she *wasn't* excited about the Haunted House.

But Mama seemed to know anyway. She floated closer to Coral and leaned down so they were eye to eye. "You don't love the Haunted House, do you?" Mama asked.

"No," Coral answered. "I can't have much fun when I'm afraid. But Angel and Shelly always want to go to the Haunted House! So I try to hide how scared I feel."

"You know, Coral," Mama said, "being scared isn't always a bad thing."

"Well, it feels like a bad thing," Coral mumbled.

"Everyone gets scared sometimes," Mama said. "I get scared when I see a great white shark swimming in Tortoise-shell Reef."

"But great white sharks are supposed to be scary!" Coral exclaimed. "They could really hurt a purrmaid!"

"Exactly!" Mama agreed. "Sometimes being afraid reminds us to be careful. That keeps us safe. You're *supposed* to be scared of dangerous things."

"But the Haunted House isn't really dangerous," Coral said. "I know that in my head. It's just that knowing the mon-sters aren't real doesn't stop me from being frightened."

Mama patted Coral's paw. "That's

normal, too," she said. "Knowing a fact can help change how we feel about something. But feelings aren't always based on what we know. Feelings come from your head *and* from your heart."

"And from your tummy," Coral said. "For me, being scared starts in my tummy." She sighed. "I want to do all the things my friends want to do, Mama. How can I do that when I'm so scared?"

Mama smiled. "You are allowed to feel however you feel. But if you want to be less scared, keep reminding yourself that you're safe at the Paw-loween Festival. And that you can count on your friends to help you if you run into any purr-oblems." She hugged Coral tight. "Have I ever told you about how your father felt at the Paw-loween Festival when he was a kitten?"

Coral shook her head.

Mama winked. "He was a total scaredy cat! He refused to even go inside the Haunted House for years and years."

Coral scratched her head. "But he goes with Shrimp every year," she said.

"Now he does," Mama said. "Do you know how he finally learned not to be so frightened?"

"No," Coral said.

"Your mother holds my paw the whole time," Papa said.

Coral spun around. "Papa! You're home!"

"I had to see your beautiful costume," Papa said, swimming up to kiss Coral's cheek. "And to ask your mother if she'll hold my paw again this year."

Mama giggled while Coral said, "Yuck! Parents aren't supposed to hold paws!" She swam to the door. "I'm leaving now. I'm going to meet Shelly and Angel in Leondra's Square. I hope they like my costume!"

"I'm sure they will!" Mama said.

"Thank you for talking to me about the Haunted House, Mama," Coral purred. "It really helped."

Mama smiled.

"We'll see you at the festival later, then," Papa said.

Coral waved goodbye and swam out. She was feeling braver than she had all day. *I just have to listen to my head instead of my heart*, she thought. *Or my tummy!*

4

It felt like she'd been waiting under the statue of Leondra fur-ever when Coral finally saw two purrmaids floating her way.

Angel was wearing a short black-and-red dress. There were eight ribbons trailing from the skirt. There was a shiny piece of sea glass on the end of each ribbon. They sparkled in the light. Shelly was wearing a very long white dress with ten longer ribbons on her skirt. There were lines of pearls on the ribbons that looked like suckers on tentacles. Right away, Coral knew that they both had squid costumes on. They looked spooky and scary.

Shelly and Angel matched each other very well. In fact, the only one who looked out of place in the group was Coral.

"Did you guys plan your costumes together?" Coral asked quietly.

"No," Shelly answered. She looked at Angel and exclaimed, "You're a vampire squid! That's tenta-cool!"

"And you're a phantom squid!" Angel replied. "How ink-credible!"

Coral wasn't sure it was ink-credible. But her friends weren't really talking to her.

Angel said, "You know, I was almost going to dress as a phantom squid!"

"And *I* was almost going to dress as a vampire squid!" Shelly said. "Can you believe how lucky this is?"

"I'm glad we made the choices that we did," Angel said.

They giggled. They didn't notice that Coral wasn't joining in.

Coral looked away quickly. She didn't

want her friends to see the disappointment on her face. Her fairy princess costume didn't match their scary squid costumes at all. She never told them she didn't want to wear a scary costume. *I figured they would already know,* she thought. But it wasn't their fault. Coral knew that.

"Hey, Coral," Angel said. "Your costume is really paw-some."

Shelly touched Coral's wings gently. "Did you make all of this yourself?"

Coral nodded. She forced herself to smile. Even though she wasn't dressed as a squid like her best friends, she was still very proud of her costume. "My favorite part is the crown," she said.

"Mine too!" Angel agreed. "I love the crystal."

"Thank you," Coral replied. Then she asked, "Should we get going?"

Shelly laughed. "Are you squidding? Of course, we should!"

※ ※ ※

Coral, Angel, and Shelly passed lots of purrmaids on their way to the Pawloween Festival. Many of them shouted nice things about the girls' costumes. But Coral got the most compliments!

Mrs. Clearwater, the director of Kittentail Cove Museum, said, "Coral, your costume is purr-ty enough to show in the museum! I especially love your crown!"

"Thank you!" Coral replied.

It was still early when the girls swam through the gates of the festival. There was a big crowd gathered in Meow Meadow already. By the end of the night, most of Kittentail Cove would stop by.

The Haunted House was an important part, but there were other activities, too.

"Should we go straight to the Haunted House?" Angel asked.

Coral shrugged. "Could we start with something else?" she asked. She hoped she wouldn't have to explain why.

Shelly and Angel nodded right away. "Of course," Angel said.

"Let's get a snack," Shelly added. Her parents, Mr. and Mrs. Lake, had a table set up with food from their restaurant.

"I love ghost eel sushi!" Angel said, plopping a piece into her mouth. After Coral and Shelly each took one, Angel grabbed another and giggled. "These are just too good!"

While the girls finished their snacks, Coral saw a lot of their classmates floating through the festival. Some were gathered around Dr. Purrdew with Paw-loween fin-go cards. Others were listening to spooky stories read by the librarians from Kittentail Cove Library.

Coral spied the Catfish Club—Umiko, Adrianna, and Cascade—dancing to "Sea Monster Mash" on the dance floor. The three of them were wearing matching peacock costumes. Usually, peacocks were blue with fancy tails made of glimmering blue, gold, and green feathers. But the Catfish Club liked lavender much more than they liked blue. Their peacock feathers were all different shades of purple. Coral thought they looked beautiful. And the peacock costumes weren't scary! Coral didn't see too many purrmaids wearing purr-ty costumes instead of spooky ones.

In fact, the only other not scary costumes Coral could see were just . . . strange. Two purrmaids wore costumes that were joined together. But each side was a land horse head and front legs! Coral had never heard of a two-headed horse.

"Is that Baker?" Shelly asked, pointing to one of the heads.

"It must be," Angel answered, "because I think the other side is Taylor."

"I wonder what their costume is supposed to be," Coral said. "Let's go find out!"

5

It seemed like Baker and Taylor were having a disagreement about something. One of the horse heads tried to stretch toward the fin-go area. The other head stretched toward the dance floor. In the end, they didn't move at all!

"Hi, Baker. Hi, Taylor," Shelly said.

"What kind of costume are you wearing?" Angel asked.

"Well, it was supposed to be a land

horse," Baker grumbled, "but Taylor wore the wrong thing."

"I did not!" Taylor shouted. "I'm wearing the front half of the horse. You were supposed to be the back half!"

"What kind of Pawloween costume would the back half of a horse be?" Baker asked.

"The kind of costume that makes sense when I'm the front half of the horse!" Taylor replied.

Baker and Taylor kept fighting about their costumes. Coral tapped Shelly's shoulder with one paw and Angel's shoulder with the other. "Let's get out of here," she whispered. "I think Baker and Taylor have lots of things to talk about!"

"And we have lots of things to do!" Angel said.

The girls giggled as they swam away. They saw their school librarian, Mr. Shippley, at the Sea Witch Pitch game. Mr. Shippley was dressed in a shark costume. His face was only visible through the shark's teeth inside the mouth.

"Hello, girls," Mr. Shippley said. "I bet you're headed to the Haunted House, aren't you?"

Coral gulped. They *were* swimming toward the Haunted House.

"It looks really great this year," Mr. Shippley continued. "I know the purrmaids who came up with all the ideas."

"You mean you and the other sea school teachers?" Coral asked.

Mr. Shippley winked. "I suppose I do. We used the jelly-o'-lanterns that you all made at school in a very special way. They look spooky!"

"We're excited to see it," Shelly said.

Mr. Shippley pointed to the Sea Witch Pitch game. There were three rows of upside-down witch hats. The row closest to the purrmaids had three hats, and they were the biggest ones. The next row had two hats that were slightly smaller. The last row was a single hat, and it was smaller than all the rest. "Would you like to play a quick game before you go?"

The girls nodded. Mr. Shippley gave them each five seashells. "Try to toss as many of these as you can into the witch hats," he said. "You get one point for each shell that falls into a hat in the first row, five points for the second row, and ten points for the last row."

Shelly went first. She got three shells inside hats. But they were all hats in the first row. "Three points, Shelly," Mr. Shippley said.

Angel missed the hats with three of her shells. But one landed in a hat in the first row and one in the second row. "Six points, Angel," Mr. Shippley said.

Coral was the last one to play. She tossed her first and second seashells . . . and they both landed in the sand. The third one hit the rim of one of the witch hats. But it bounced the wrong way and landed in the sand, too.

"Two more tries, Coral," Angel said.

"You can do it!" Shelly added.

Coral took a deep breath. She tossed

another shell—and it landed inside a hat in the first row! "One point, Coral!" Mr. Shippley said. "Let's see what you can do with the last one. You could still win!"

Coral knew she probably wouldn't win. Even if she scored another point, she'd still have the fewest points overall. But she still had to take her turn. She concentrated on the witch hat closest to her. Then she closed her eyes and tossed the shell. She kept her eyes closed until she heard her friends shriek.

"What happened?" Coral asked.

"You got ten points!" Mr. Shippley exclaimed. He pulled her seashell out of the witch hat in the last row. "That means you have eleven points."

"Which means you won!" Shelly said.

"I can't believe it!" Angel added. "But Shelly is right. You won, fair and square."

Coral grinned so hard her cheeks hurt. "I can't believe it, either!" she said, laughing.

"Do you girls want to play again?" Mr. Shippley asked. "Or do you want to get to the Haunted House?"

Angel and Shelly looked at Coral. "Well, Coral?" Angel asked.

Coral felt very lucky after winning Sea Witch Pitch. *Maybe I'll get lucky again and the Haunted House won't be too scary,* she thought. "I think meow's the time!" Coral said. "Haunted House, here we come!"

6

The line for the Haunted House reached to the far end of the building. Luckily, there were lots of things to see while they were waiting.

The building itself was shaped like a long, thin rectangle. There were windows all along the walls. There was something glowing in each of the windows. "Our jelly-o'-lanterns!" Angel exclaimed. She pointed to the closest one. "Here's mine!"

"It looks great," Coral said. "Can you see Shelly's? Or mine?"

"Not yet," Angel said, "but there are a lot of windows left!"

Coral, Angel, and Shelly got to see all the creepy and cool faces their class-mates had created. "These really are paw-some," Shelly said. She pointed to two jelly-o'-lanterns next to each other and giggled. "These two look like my twin sisters when they're angry!"

Coral pointed to a different jelly-o'-lantern. "And this one looks like my little brother, Shrimp, when he's whining!"

The girls continued to move through the line, swimming past more windows. Angel spotted Shelly's jelly-o'-lantern in the last window before the entrance to the Haunted House. But they couldn't find Coral's jelly-o'-lantern anywhere!

Coral frowned. "Maybe Ms. Harbor forgot?" she wondered.

"Or maybe there are more jelly-o'-lanterns inside the Haunted House," Shelly said.

Coral shrugged. "It doesn't matter," she mumbled.

The girls didn't have a chance to keep looking for Coral's jelly-o'-lantern. They reached the front of the line. Someone was floating there in a ghost costume. He had a white sheet over his head with two small holes for eyes. Even though they couldn't see his face, the girls knew exactly who it was. That's because the ghost was wearing a top hat—the same hat that Mayor Rivers wore every day!

"Hi, Mayor Rivers," Angel said. "Great costume!"

"How did you know it was me?" Mayor Rivers asked.

The girls smiled. "Just a lucky guess," Angel replied.

"Hmmph," Mayor Rivers huffed. Then he said, "Here's what you need to know about the Haunted House." He handed Angel a small lantern. It was filled with glow-in-the-dark plankton. "Take one of these for your group," he said. "It can get a little dark inside the Haunted House."

Coral felt a shiver run up her spine. *Maybe this isn't a good idea,* she thought.

Shelly and Angel didn't seem to be worried. They were listening closely to Mayor Rivers. "There is only one path through the Haunted House," he continued. "So don't go backward—just move from one room to the next. If you get lost, look down at the sand. We've marked your way with these." He held out a small sea urchin shell that had been painted orange.

"It looks like a mini pumpkin," Coral purred.

"Purr-fect for Paw-loween," Mayor Rivers said, nodding. "You should also know that there is a special surprise for everyone who is brave enough to make it all the way through."

"Really?" Angel asked. Her eyes grew wide.

Mayor Rivers nodded again. "But if you need to leave the Haunted House for any reason, there are exits in many of the rooms. Just find a door marked with a glow-in-the-dark sign that says BOO and you'll be back outside, safe and sound."

"But if you leave, you don't get the special surprise, right?" Coral asked.

"Exactly!" Mayor Rivers said. He opened the front door. "Have fun, girls!"

Coral gulped. *What if I can't have fun?*

7

Angel and Shelly swam into the Haunted House. Coral followed—she just moved a little more slowly than her friends.

Mayor Rivers closed the door behind the girls. It got really dark right away. Coral inched closer to Angel, who held the lantern up. "I'm glad Mayor Rivers gave this to us," Angel whispered.

Coral nodded.

The girls swam forward into the first

room. Luckily, it was much brighter in there. Angel lowered the lantern.

The room was mostly empty. There was just one thing at the far end. It was right in front of the way out. At first, Coral wasn't sure if it was a statue or a purrmaid in a costume. The only thing she knew for sure was that it was . . . a monster!

"Eek!" Coral shrieked. She hid behind her friends.

"It's all right, Coral," Angel whispered. "It's just a decoration."

"You don't know that!" Coral replied.

Shelly pointed down at the orange sea urchin shells. They were easy to see in the sand on the ocean floor. They led past the monster to a doorway. "This is the way they want us to go," Shelly whispered. "That means it's safe."

Angel nodded. "I agree," she purred.

Coral floated behind her friends as they followed the shells. Soon, they could see the monster more clearly. It was wrapped head to tail in bandages. There was a small gap where Coral could see some eyes. But otherwise, even the monster's mouth was covered. Maybe that's why the only sounds she heard were some moans.

"It's not a statue!" Coral said. She knew deep down that the monster was really a purrmaid from town. It was probably even someone she knew! But that didn't stop her from trembling.

"It's a mer-mummy!" Angel said. "What a great costume!"

"I can't tell who it is," Shelly added.

There was no way to get out of the room without swimming right past the mer-mummy. Coral didn't want to get any closer to the monster. But she didn't want to stay in the room, either!

Coral tried not to look at the monster's face as she swam. But just when she had passed the monster, she heard, "OOOOOOOO!" To make things worse, the monster tapped Coral's shoulder!

Coral gulped. There was no way she was going to turn around. Instead, she darted forward and ended up in front of her friends.

"Whoa!" Angel said. "What's going on?"

"No time to explain!" Coral cried, grabbing her friends' paws. "Come with me!"

She dragged Angel and Shelly through the doorway. She wanted to get away from the monster! But she didn't get very far! All of a sudden, it stopped being easy to move quickly. That's because there were creepy clumps of kelp in the way. She had to push past them. She swam slowly until something wrapped around her tail! She looked down and hoped it wasn't a new monster. *It's just kelp,* she thought.

Angel squealed. "There's something on my paw!"

Coral pulled the kelp away. "It's all right, Angel," she purred. "I got kelp on me, too."

"This is so spooky!" Shelly said.

"Do you see the orange shells?" Coral asked. "Which way do we go?"

"I see them," Angel said. "Come with me."

Angel took Coral's paw, and Coral took Shelly's paw. Then Angel led all three of them through the kelp toward a long, skinny door. At least, it looked like a door from far away. When Coral looked at the orange shells in the sand, she frowned. They made a path that turned off to the side.

The girls swam forward. They seemed to get closer to the door. Then Coral realized something. "It's a mirror!" she exclaimed. But it wasn't a regular mirror. When the girls saw their reflections, they looked stretched out like they were much taller than they really were.

"This is so weird," Angel said. "But I look good taller!"

Shelly and Coral
laughed. Then Coral
noticed something.
She swam up to the
mirror to take a
closer look. Then
she wailed, "Oh no!
The crystal fell out of
my princess crown."
She looked all around.
"I don't see it anywhere!"

"Do you want to go back
and look for it?" Shelly asked.

Coral bit her lip. There was no way
she wanted to swim through all that kelp
again. Or see that monster! She took
another look in the mirror. The crown
still looked purr-ty.

But then Coral spied something in

the corner of the mirror. It was the mer-mummy's hand! *It's following us!* she thought. *We have to get out of here!*

"Let's go!" Coral cried. She dragged her friends to the next room.

"What are you doing, Coral?" Shelly asked.

"The mer-mummy! It's right behind us!" Coral replied.

Angel and Shelly checked over their shoulders. "There's no one there," Angel said.

Coral spun around. Angel was right! She couldn't see anyone. "Maybe the monster is hiding in the kelp?" she suggested.

Shelly and Angel giggled for a second. They stopped almost immediately. "We're not laughing at you, Coral," Angel began.

"That was just a nervous laugh," Shelly added.

Coral looked away. Maybe her friends didn't mean to laugh at her. But it felt like that was exactly what they were doing. *I have to be braver,* she thought.

Shelly floated over to hold Coral's paw. "I think you just imagined it."

Coral frowned. "Maybe," she said.

"I see an exit door," Angel said. She pointed to the glowing BOO sign to their left. "Do you want to leave?"

Coral shook her head. "I'm not going to be a scaredy cat," she said. "We can keep going."

"Are you sure?" Angel asked.

Coral *wasn't* sure. But she didn't want anyone to laugh at her again. So she nodded and said, "Let's go."

8

The next room of the Haunted House was dark. But Coral was happy that there weren't kelp clumps everywhere. Angel raised the lantern again so the girls could look around.

At first, the room looked empty. But then Coral saw something moving near the wall. She swam a bit closer—and then immediately jumped back. "Eek!" she cried. There were things crawling all over the walls! "Sea spiders!" Coral said.

"I hate sea spiders!" Angel cried. "Can we move to the next room?"

Coral nodded. Shelly rolled her eyes and said, "Fine, we can leave. But you know that sea spiders only eat things like jellyfish and sea sponges, right? They don't eat purrmaids."

"Let's not test that," Angel said.

The girls followed the orange shells again. This time, they were led into a long and narrow hallway. It looked empty— but Coral knew that didn't mean it really was empty. She looked carefully at the walls again, checking for sea spiders.

The purrmaids swam slowly. At first, there wasn't anything scary. Then, suddenly, a black cloud of ink surrounded them.

"I can't see!" Angel yelped.

"It's squid ink," Shelly shrieked, "and I think it's staining my costume!"

Coral bit her lip to keep from giggling. Shelly hated getting dirty! Only Shelly would be afraid of stains!

The girls swam a little farther. And they got hit with another cloud of ink!

"I don't want to be in this room!" Shelly exclaimed.

For the first time in the Haunted House, Coral realized that everyone was afraid of something. *But Angel and Shelly are definitely not scaredy cats,* she thought. *I need their help to be brave some of the time, but they need my help to be brave sometimes, too.*

"Stay behind me, Shelly," Coral said. "I'll keep the ink from getting on you."

"Thank you, Coral," Shelly said.

The three friends only faced one more puff of ink before they made it through the hallway. There was a sign at the entrance of the next room that read CAVE OF THE SEA MONSTERS. It was the biggest room in the Haunted House so far.

There were tanks set up along the walls of the cave. The girls floated to the first tank. Angel held the lantern close to the glass. Soon, they saw a black-and-red squid inside. "Angel, look!" Coral said. "It's you!"

"You're right!" Shelly agreed. "Angel looks just like that vampire squid."

Angel grinned. "Let's see what's over here."

There was another squid inside the next tank. But it was not a vampire squid. It was a long white squid with even longer tentacles. "This one is a phantom squid like you, Shelly!" Angel said.

"This must be a baby," Shelly purred. "Grown-up phantom squids can be thirty feet long."

The next few tanks held hagfish, witch eels, and sea dragons. Coral thought the hagfish and witch eels were creepy. But the sea dragons were graceful and fancy.

The last tank was the biggest one. There were about a dozen white jellyfish with flowy tentacles in the tank. They gently floated around.

"I think these are ghost jellyfish," Coral said.

The girls pushed their noses against the glass to get a better look. They watched quietly for a moment. "They really do look like ghosts," Shelly said softly.

Angel snorted. "Ghosts aren't real!"

"You know," Coral said, "I thought all these animals would be scary. And some of them are. But others are actually really beautiful." She focused on one jellyfish that floated toward the left side of the tank. Coral swam next to it. She wasn't paying attention to anything else. That's why she didn't realize Angel was in the way—until she crashed into her friend!

"Oof!" Angel yelped. She got knocked into the sand. She slid along the ocean floor. The paw holding the lantern hit the ground.

"Sorry!" Coral exclaimed.

"Is your paw all right, Angel?" Shelly asked.

"I think so," Angel answered.

"It's not all right," Coral gasped.

Angel waved her paw right and left. "No, I think it's fine," she said.

"I'm not talking about your paw," Coral said. She pointed at the lantern. It was cracked! The plankton were spilling out. As they did, the light got dimmer and dimmer.

"What are we going to do?" Shelly asked. "That was our only light!"

"I don't know," Angel replied. "But we need to figure it out!"

It's my fault, Coral thought. *I have to think of something!*

9

Coral, Angel, and Shelly looked at each other. But it was already getting hard to see.

"The orange shells!" Coral exclaimed suddenly. "We can still follow them to get through the Haunted House."

"That's a great idea!" Angel said. She looked down at the ocean floor. "Umm," Angel said, "I'm having a hard time seeing the shells."

"It's very dark," Shelly said. She bent down to get closer to the sand. "I don't see any shells."

"Maybe when I got knocked over," Angel said, "I pushed the shells away by accident."

Coral frowned. "That probably happened," she said. "But there were a lot of shells. We should still be able to find the trail."

Coral and Angel bent down next to Shelly. They all tried to spot anything orange—without moving too much. None of the girls wanted to get too far away in the dark! But they couldn't find anything.

Coral took a deep breath. Then she said, "You two stay here. I'm going to swim a bit to look for the orange shells."

"We can look, too," Shelly suggested. "That way we can check in three different directions."

Coral shook her head. "It would be too easy to get turned around in the dark. It's better if you stay where you are." She gulped. "I'll be quick."

Coral began to swim away. She kept her eyes on the sand. Luckily, she didn't have to go far before she spied an orange mini pumpkin in the sand! "I found one!" she cried. "I'm coming to get you two!"

"Yay!" Angel and Shelly cheered.

Coral turned around and then reached down to the ocean floor. She stuck a claw in the ground, right next to the shell. As she swam back toward her friends, she used her claw to draw a line in the sand. That way, they wouldn't have to search for the right path again!

"Keep talking," Coral shouted. "I can follow the sound to get to you."

"Coral is full of paw-some ideas!" Angel yelled, laughing.

"Yes, she is!" Shelly added.

They made so much noise that it was easy for Coral to find the way to her friends. Soon, she could see them, lit by a faint light.

Then Coral realized, *I shouldn't be able to see Angel and Shelly! Our lantern is broken!* She gasped. *Where is that light coming from?*

The light moved closer to Shelly and Angel. Someone was clearly swimming their way, holding a lantern. They couldn't see who it was because their backs were turned.

It must be another group of purrmaids coming through the Haunted House, Coral thought. But then the light was close enough that Coral could see that it was held by . . . a bandaged paw!

"The mer-mummy!" Coral shouted. She raced forward and grabbed her friends by the paws.

"What?" Shelly yelped. But Coral was already dragging her away in the darkness.

"The mer-mummy is chasing us," Coral hissed. "Come on!"

"But where are we going?" Angel asked. "I can't see anything!"

Coral stopped. Angel was right. If they just swam without know- ing where to go, they could get lost. Or they could swim right into the mer-mummy!

Out of the corner of her eye, Coral saw something glowing. "I see the exit!" she yelled.

"Let's go!" Shelly said.

The mer-mummy's lantern was getting closer. The girls moved toward the BOO sign. But just as they were about to push the door open, Coral froze. "We can't," she said.

"Why?" Shelly and Angel both asked.

"The Cave of the Sea Monsters is the last room in the Haunted House," Coral said. "That means I got all the way through the house. I don't want to give up this close to the special surprise." She sighed. "Besides, there's nothing at the Paw-loween Festival that would actually hurt us. It may look scary, but it's not really scary."

The mer-mummy was close enough now that the girls could hear it moaning, "OOOOOOO!" The purrmaids turned toward the sound, holding each other's paws tightly.

"I've been brave this long because you two have been here for me," Coral

whispered. "If we stick together, we don't
have to be afraid of the mer-mummy."

Coral couldn't see Shelly or Angel.
But she could tell that they were nodding. Together, they watched the lantern get closer until they could see the
mer-mummy clearly. It reached up and
grabbed the bandages on its face. *I won't*

show how scared I am! Coral thought. *Or, at least, I'll do my best not to show how scared I am!*

Coral tried to be brave. She really, really did. But her imagination filled her head with ideas of how terrible the mer-mummy might look. She couldn't help herself. She squeezed her eyes shut.

"Hey, Coral," a voice purred, "are you all right?"

The voice sounded very familiar. Coral opened one eye. Then she gasped. "Ms. Harbor!" she exclaimed. "It's you!"

10

"We didn't recognize you, Ms. Harbor," Shelly said.

"That's purr-ty clear," Ms. Harbor replied. "It's nice to be able to talk again! Those bandages were like a muzzle." She turned to Coral. "You dropped your crystal when you came in. I didn't want you to lose it."

Ms. Harbor held her paw out. Coral

saw the crystal from her crown glittering in Ms. Harbor's palm.

"You were following us to give me this?" Coral asked. Her mouth dropped open.

"You didn't think I was just coming to scare you, did you?" Ms. Harbor answered.

Coral giggled. "Well, I *did* think that," she said. "I can't believe it was you the whole time, Ms. Harbor! I was afraid for nothing!"

Angel and Shelly nodded in agreement.

"Then why didn't you girls go out through the exit?" Ms. Harbor asked.

Coral shrugged. "When we realized that we were all scared, it made us feel a little better." Her friends nodded again. "It was easier to be brave once we knew it was all right to feel afraid."

"I'm very proud of you," Ms. Harbor said. "It isn't easy for grown-ups to face their fears. You girls did exactly that." She smiled. "It seems that even though I didn't give you any homework tonight, you three managed to learn something very important."

"I'm very proud of us, too," Coral said.

"But I don't want to try to be this brave again until at least next Paw-loween!"

Everyone laughed. Then Ms. Harbor said, "I think you kittens have earned the special surprise. Let's go!"

Ms. Harbor knew the way through the Haunted House, so she easily led everyone back to the path marked by the orange shells. They followed the path out to a courtyard. There, they found a huge table coral. It held bowls and bowls of Paw-loween candy—blowfish pops, fur-shey bars, sandy corn, butterfishers, anem&m's, and so much more!

"I've never seen this much candy!" Angel exclaimed.

"They even have three meows-keteers bars!" Shelly added. "These are really hard to find."

Angel and Shelly grabbed pawfuls of

candy. But Coral hadn't moved yet. She was staring at something else in the middle of the table. It was a cake stand, but it didn't hold a cake. Instead, there was a pumpkin jellyfish on it. The pumpkin jellyfish had a small triangle for a nose, two circles for eyes, and two triangles for ears. The smiling mouth was shaped like a W. On the triangle ears, there were earrings painted on.

The jelly-o'-lantern looked just like Ms. Harbor.

"Is that my jelly-o'-lantern?" Coral asked.

Ms. Harbor grinned. "I told you it was purr-fect. I knew the moment I saw it that I wanted it to have this special place on the treat table." She floated closer to the table and waved for Coral to follow. "I realized later that the Haunted House

isn't your favorite thing. I was worried that you wouldn't get to see what I did with your jelly-o'-lantern. I am so happy you made it all the way through the house." She squeezed Coral's paw. "I am proud of how brave you were tonight. And I'm very proud of your art talent!"

Coral felt her face getting warm.

Ms. Harbor's words made her feel really good. "I'm glad I got through the Haunted House, too." She floated over to Shelly and Angel. "I couldn't have done it without my friends."

"And you never have to!" Shelly said.

"Uh agwee!" Angel added. Her mouth was so full of sea-nut-butter cups that Coral couldn't understand her words.

"What did you say, Angel?" Coral asked.

Angel swallowed the candy. "I said, 'I agree!'"

Everyone laughed.

"Enjoy the treats, girls," Ms. Harbor said. "I have to get back to my spot— there are more purrmaids to scare!"

"Excuse me, Ms. Harbor," Coral whispered. "Can I ask you something?" She pulled her teacher away from her friends.

"Of course, Coral," Ms. Harbor replied softly. "What is it?"

Coral bent down and scooped up three of the orange sea urchin shells. "Is it all right if I take three of these?" she asked.

"Do you want them for your bracelets?" Ms. Harbor asked.

Coral nodded.

"I think that's a paw-some idea," Ms. Harbor whispered.

"Are you two planning a Paw-loween trick?" Angel asked.

Coral turned to smile at her friends. She floated closer. "Not at all," she said, giggling. "It's much  more of a Paw-loween treat!" She held out the orange shells. "Ms. Harbor says we can have these for our friendship bracelets."

"These are purr-fect," Shelly said.

"You had a fin-tastic idea, Coral," Angel added.

Coral pulled Shelly and Angel into a group hug. "Thank you for being here for me tonight. You helped me be brave. Now I'm afraid of only one thing."

"What is it?" Angel asked.

"And how can we help?" Shelly added.

They both looked worried until Coral grinned. "I'm scared," she said, "that Angel might have eaten all the butterfishers!"

It's Angel's birthday ... but her friends don't seem to want to celebrate! Is her special day ruined?

Turn the page for a sneak peek!

Angel put her new birthday hat into a bag. She wanted her friends to be the first purrmaids in Kittentail Cove to see it!

Soon, Angel was swimming toward Leondra's Square. She decided to go to Coral's house first. As she passed the window, she heard some voices. She peeked through the glass—and saw Coral with another purrmaid. It was Shelly!

What is Shelly doing at Coral's house? Angel wondered. She waved at her friends. But they didn't notice. They were hunched over something on the counter and had their backs to the window. Angel could tell they were looking at it closely. Shelly pointed, and Coral nodded. Then they both laughed.

Angel frowned. Coral didn't really look like she was studying. And Shelly definitely wasn't napping. She didn't know what they were doing. But she did know that her best friends clearly didn't want to be with her on her birthday.

Angel didn't want Shelly and Coral to see that she was there. She floated down to the floor and out of sight. She didn't really know what to do next.

Mommy said she should talk things out with her friends. *But how am I supposed to talk to them about this?* Angel thought. *They made up a story so they wouldn't have to spend the afternoon with me. And it's my birthday!*

Angel was trying to decide if she wanted to talk to her friends when she heard Coral's front door opening. She ducked behind a large kelp bush. Shelly and Coral swam past. They were so busy talking that they didn't even look in Angel's direction.

"I'm so glad we convinced Angel to go home after school," Coral purred.

"This will be so much easier without her," Shelly agreed.

Angel gulped. *I never knew they wanted to get rid of me,* she thought. She felt tears welling in her eyes.

Then Coral said, "This is going to be so much fun!"

"I know!" Shelly exclaimed. "I wish we had thought about doing this a long time ago!"

As the purrmaids swam farther away, Angel realized she wasn't just feeling sad. She was also feeling a little angry. *If they don't like something about me,* she thought, *why don't they just tell me?* Angel never meant to be annoying. But it wasn't very friendly for Coral and Shelly to make up a story just to get away from her!

Angel clenched her paws. She was going to find out what was so important to Shelly and Coral that they would treat her like this. *I'm going to follow them,* she thought.

Angel popped ou
kelp. She didn't want
that she was there. S
idea! She took her bin
bag. She remembered
said about the hat hic
that would be useful.